DEDICATION

To all the early year's families I have been privileged to share musical journeys with

Mattie & Mimi's Musical Adventures - Winter

Mattie & Mimi Monkeys' Musical Adventures - Winter

By Donna Fordham

Illustrations by Jennifer Tucker

Mattie & Mimi's Musical Adventures – Winter

CONTENTS

ACKNOWLEDGMENTS

To the many artists & musicians who have so generously shared their knowledge and ideas

Mattie & Mimi's Musical Adventures - Winter

1 SNOW IS FALLING

Mattie & Mimi monkey love to copy interesting sounds
As the snow fell in the garden they closed their eyes and placed their fingers on their lips (*Shhhh*)
to hear the snow fall gently on the ground (*sploosh, sploosh*).
As they watched and listened to the falling snow they began to sing:

(tune of London Bridge is falling down)

Snow is falling on the ground, on the ground,

on the ground

Snow is falling on the ground, now its winter

2 WIND IS BLOWING

The snow fell faster and the snowflakes blew (*wooosh*)

Swirling high in the air before landing on the grass,

trees and rooftops (*sploosh*)

Mattie & Mimi monkey continued their song:

Wind is blowing snow around, snow around,

Snow around

Wind is blowing snow around, now its winter

3 SCRAPE THE SNOW

The monkeys wanted to go outside to experience the
snow,
Mattie & Mimi monkey pulled up their coat zips
(*zzzzzzip*) and put on their scarves, gloves and boots.
In the frosty garden the snow fell on their faces (*brrrrr*)
it was cold.
They stamped footprints walking around on the snow
covered grass (*stomp, stomp, stomp*)
Mimi scooped some snow into her gloved hands and
sung:

Scrape the snow into a mound, to a mound

to a mound

Scrape the snow into a mound

Now it's winter

4 LET'S BUILD A SNOWMAN

The monkeys formed a small snowball to cup in their hands. They decided to roll it on the snowy ground (*squish, squish*) to make it bigger. As they rolled it all around in the snow the snowball grew into a large round snowy ball. It was big enough to build a snowman. The monkeys started to sing:

Let's build a snowman, let's make him fat
Give him a round head and put on a hat
A carrot for his nose and then I suppose
Some buttons down his chest
Oh he really is the best
Cos he's a fat, jolly snowman
A roly poly snowman

We've made a snowman today, Hooray!

5 SNOW IS MELTING

The monkeys came inside to warm up (*Ahhh*) and looked out of the window to see the snowman standing proud in the garden with his red hat, his two black shiny stone eyes, his orange carrot nose and his two brown twig arms. They waved (*yoohoo*) to him and blew kisses until it was too dark to see him anymore.

In the morning the sun was shining and Mattie & Mimi monkey felt excited to see their friendly snowman, they glanced out of their window but could only see the red hat and 2 twigs. The warm sun had melted all the snow in the garden and took their snowy friend away.

The monkeys felt a little sad but knew that the best way to cheer themselves up was to sing:

Sun has melted snow away, snow away, snow away
Sun has melted snow away, now it's warmer

ABOUT THE AUTHOR

Donna Fordham spent her early adult years as a family lawyer in Great Yarmouth & Lowestoft. She also enjoyed working at Elm Tree Primary School Lowestoft. After having her 2 children Henry & Hattie she combined her role as mother with in practice training as an early year's music educator. She was privileged to work alongside some pioneering artists at The Priory Children's Centre. She has been offering music classes for parents with their babies, toddlers and pre-school children for over 10 years. She enjoys playing her ukulele, dancing, reading and making friends.

ABOUT THE ILLUSTRATOR

Jennifer Tucker (M.A; B.A Hons.P.G.C.E) taught preschool children in the 70's and after study at UEA lectured students in History, Media & Communications for 25 years at Great Yarmouth College. Since retirement in 2006 she has enjoyed different art, heritage and music projects.

When approached to by Donna for some illustrations Jennifer was happy to take on the challenge during lockdown 2021. She believes that learning never stops; so in her 80th year, gained some more mixed media and technology skills in order to illustrate this book.

Printed in Great Britain
by Amazon